THIS BOOK BELONGS TO

_____

To my poop obsessed babies

Love you so much.

Mummy x o x o

Percy the pooping penguin

A true story (kind of)

Luna James

This is Percy. He may seem cute, cuddly, and clumsy, but don't be fooled. He is a feisty little fellow.

My grandma warned me,

"BEWARE, MY DEAR, THE ADÉLIE SPECIES, FOR THEY ARE PRONE TO SHOOT THEIR FECES."

A penguin that shoots poop? How could this be? I hear you ask.

Yep, a poop-shooting penguin, or a guano-making machine, to be more precise.

"Guano" is a word used for all the accumulated poop.

In Adélie penguins, it is pink because of their **krill**-rich diet.

The male Adélie penguins, aka brush-tailed penguins, are the nest builders.

Percy is in competition with the other guys. Whoever has the biggest and best nest attracts the female.

Percy collects rocks and rolls them back to his nest.

Sometimes he even steals rocks from the other penguin dudes.

Luckily, Percy's nest has just about passed the female test!

Once the two eggs have been laid both parents take it in turns to incubate.

Whoever is left with the eggs are not allowed to leave, no matter what.

Not even to poop? I hear you ask.
Yep, not even to poop.

Projectile pooping is the answer. A poop bomb
ensures that the nest stays nice and clean.

Uh oh, nature calls!
Percy needs to go poop.

Percy has pooped so much that NASA had to be sent to space to investigate.

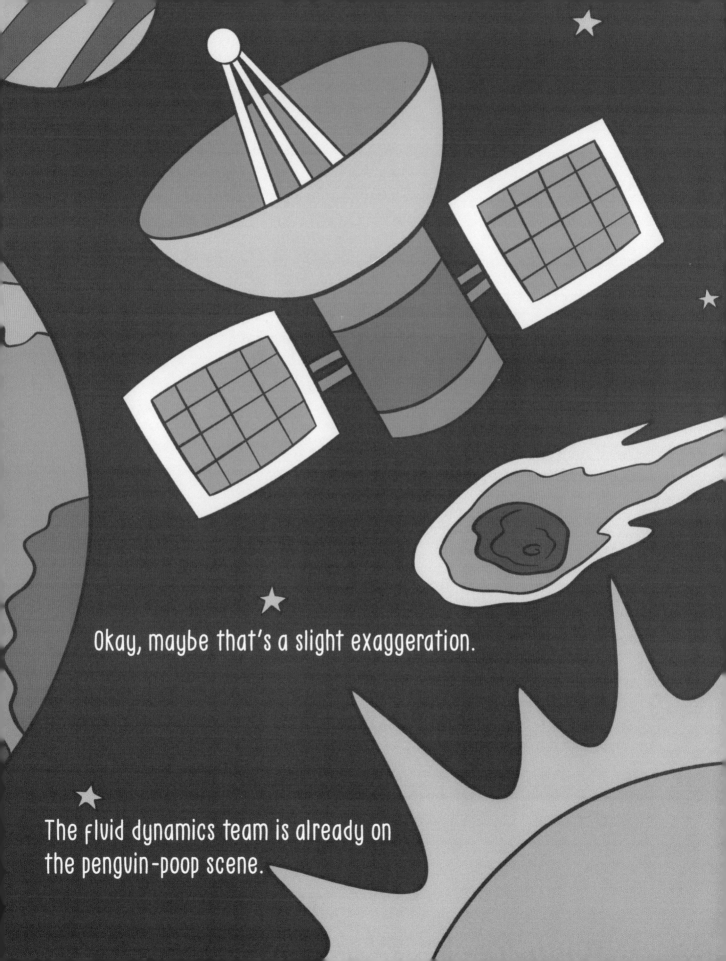

Okay, maybe that's a slight exaggeration.

The fluid dynamics team is already on the penguin-poop scene.

They're learning all sorts of valuable science stuff from the guano. In fact, humans have been monitoring penguin poop from space for over thirty years.

Antarctica is covered in

pink penguin poop.

Who would have thought?

It stains everything. Colonies that humans would have never otherwise known about have been detected using satellites.

Actual image from space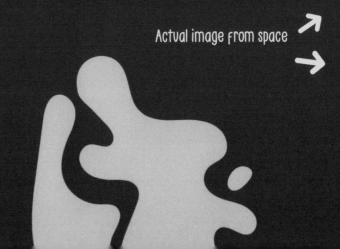

Heronia Island

Beagle Island

Darwin Island

Brash Island

Poop can tell a whole story: the number of penguins in the colony, population trends, and their diet.

It can even indicate the condition of wildlife around them.

Simply put, penguin poop is awesome stuff. It's also a highly effective fertilizer for humans.

Grandma was right when she said,

"HUMANS ARE WEIRD; THIS I KNOW IS TRUE. THEY ARE COMPLETELY OBSESSED WITH PENGUIN POO."

Human (Homo sapien)

Something else I have learned from personal experience is that Adélie penguin poop is a deterrent for predators.

Percy has definitely been eating plenty of
krill!

Please consider leaving a review.

Thanks so much :)

Luna

You can find my other books on

amazon

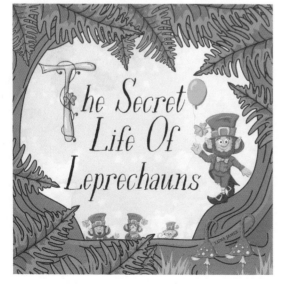

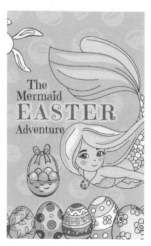

Printed in Great Britain
by Amazon

20849270R00022